GW00862900

ISAAC BASHEVIS SINGER

Shrewd Todie
and
Lyzer the Miser

& OTHER CHILDREN'S STORIES

Illustrated by
MARGOT ZEMACH

BAREFOOT BOOKS
Boston & Bath
1994

Barefoot Books
Horticultural Hall
300 Massachusetts Avenue
Boston, Massachusetts 02115

Series designed by Dede Cummings

9 8 7 6 5 4 3 2 1

First Barefoot Books Edition
Printed in Singapore on acid-free paper ⊗
Distributed in the United States by Random House,
Inc., and in Canada by Random House of Canada Ltd

See page 157 for Library of Congress
Cataloging-in-Publication data.

CONTENTS

CONTENTS

EDITOR'S FOREWORD

I t is said that when the Baal Shem Tov, the founder of Hasidism, saw misfortune threatening his people, he would go to a special place in the forest where he would meditate, light a fire, say a prayer, and the trouble would be averted. Years later, one of his disciples went to that special place in the forest, but didn't know how to light the fire, so he said the prayer, and, again, the danger was averted. Still later, another disciple, who knew neither how to light the fire nor how to say the prayer, saved his people because he at least could locate the secret place in the forest. But finally, years after that, another disciple spoke to God and said, "I am unable to light the fire. I do not know how to say the prayer. I can't even find the place in the forest. All I can do is tell the story, and this must be sufficient." And it was sufficient.

At the Yad Vashem holocaust memorial in Jerusalem, it is written, "Remembrance is the secret of redemption. Forgetfulness leads to exile." And it was the gift and calling of the Yiddish writer Isaac Bashevis Singer (1904–1991) to remember, re-create, and pass down to us in a dying language some of the greatest and most revivifying wisdom stories of our century. They are stories that remind us of the way we were and of who we truly are and that illustrate the psychologist James Hillman's notion of the story as "something lived in and lived through, a way in which the soul finds itself in life."

The child of a Hasidic rabbi father and a devout but more rationalist mother, Isaac Singer grew up on Krochmalna Street in Warsaw, Poland, immersed in the folklore and legends of the Jewish shtetls and settlements of Eastern Europe—a fantastic world of angels and demons, *dybbuks* and golems, goblins and ghosts. "In our home," the author once recalled, "there was always talk about spirits of the dead that possess the bodies of the living, souls reincarnated as animals, houses inhabited by hobgoblins, cellars haunted by demons. My father spoke of these things, first of all because he was interested in them, and second because . . . it [was] necessary to remind [children] from time to time that there are still mysterious forces at work in the world." Isaac's mother also contributed to her son's imaginative life by acceding to his continual requests for bedtime stories about schnooks, shlemiels, shlemazels, and other simpletons (mostly from Chelm, the proverbial city of fools), stories that Isaac's mother had learned from her own mother and grandmother.

Years later in his self-imposed American exile, the author summoned up and recorded his remembrances of the past in various furnished rooms in Brooklyn and in the cafeterias of Manhattan's Lower East Side. As the critic Irving Howe noted, Singer wrote of the decimated cities, towns, and villages of his childhood "as if they were still there," describing them in extraordinary novels and stories like *The Magician of Lublin*, *The Family Moscat*, "Gimpel the Fool," and "Yentl the

Yeshiva Boy," which first appeared in the Yiddish newspaper the *Jewish Daily Forward*. "I keep going back to 10 Krochmalna Street in my writing," Singer said. "I remember every little corner and every person there. I say to myself that just as other people are digging gold which God has created billions of years ago, my literary gold mine is this street. I keep on returning to it with the feeling that there are still treasures which I haven't used up." For Singer, home was like the Tao, "used but never used up, hidden but always present." And indeed he unknowingly followed the advice of an ancient Chinese sage. "Just remember where you come from: this is the essence of wisdom."

It wasn't until the author was sixty-two years old that he was persuaded by one of his editors to try his hand at writing for children. It was an inspired suggestion; the result was *Zlateh the Goat and Other Stories* (1966), the first of Singer's fourteen storybooks for young people.

"I like to write for children," he once declared. "You can't be a faker when you write for them. Children don't care how famous you are or what the critics say about you." And he added, "They still like clarity, logic, and even such obsolete stuff as punctuation. Even more, the young reader demands a real story, with a beginning, a middle, and an end, the way stories have been told for thousands of years. . . . Children are by nature inclined to mysticism. They believe in God, in the Devil, in good spirits and bad spirits, and in all kinds of magic. Yet they require true consistency in these stories. There is often great logic in religion and there is little logic in materialism. Those who maintain that the world created itself are often people without any respect for reason." Finally, he asserted what might be taken as his credo: "Without folklore and deep roots in a specific soil, literature must decline and wither away. This is true in all literature of all times. Luckily, children's literature is even now more rooted in folklore than the literature for adults. And this alone makes children's literature so important in our generation."

When he wrote for children, Singer often retold the stories he had remembered from his mother when he was young, though he "re-created" them, as he said, "in plot, detail, and perspective." (A Tuscan proverb states, "A tale is not beautiful if nothing is added to it.") In one of his children's tales,

"Naftali the Storyteller and His Horse, Sus," Singer conveys the passionate, spiritual nature of his own vocation. As a child, we are told, Naftali loves stories "too much," demanding at least one tale from his mother every night. "At times she had to tell him two or three stories before he would close his eyes. He always demanded, 'Mama, more, more!'" When Naftali grows up, he obtains a horse-drawn wagon filled only with storybooks, and he travels from town to town selling his beloved volumes or reciting his mesmerizing tales to children and adults alike. "Naftali," Singer informs us, "had decided on something else too—to become a writer of storybooks. . . . Each person had his or her own manner of speaking. Reb Zebulun [the boy's mentor and guru] told Naftali, 'When a day passes, it is no longer there. What remains of it? Nothing more than a story. If stories weren't told or books weren't written, man would live like the beasts, only for the day. . . . Today we live, but by tomorrow today will be a story. The whole world, all human life, is one long story.' "

The world may have forgotten the location of the secret place in the forest, how to light the ritual fire, how to say the necessary prayer; but in his incomparable stories for children and adults, Singer remembers to remember what has been lost. And by doing so, he redeems us.

The stories in this collection first appeared in two volumes: *When Shlemiel Went to Warsaw and Other Stories* (1968) and *Naftali the Storyteller and His Horse, Sus, and Other Stories* (1976). (The author dedicated the first of these books to "the memory of my father and mother—great and enthusiastic story-tellers, persons of deep faith and love of man, especially of all Shlemiels, old and young.") "Shrewd Todie and Lyzer the Miser," "Tsirtsur and Peziza," "Utzel and His Daughter Poverty," "Menaseh's Dream," and "When Shlemiel Went to Warsaw" are taken from the first volume; "Lemel and Tzipa," "The Cat Who Thought She Was a Dog and the Dog Who Thought He Was a Cat," and "Naftali the Storyteller and His Horse, Sus" are taken from the second, with the original black-and-white drawings by Margot Zemach.

JONATHAN COTT
Series Editor

SHREWD TODIE
and
LYZER THE MISER

I n a village somewhere in the Ukraine there lived a poor man called Todie. Todie had a wife, Shaindel, and seven children, but he could never earn enough to feed them properly. He tried many trades and failed in all of them. It was said of Todie that if he decided to deal in candles the sun would never set. He was nicknamed Shrewd Todie because whenever he managed to make some money, it was always by trickery.

This winter was an especially cold one. The snowfall was heavy and Todie had no money to buy wood for the stove. His seven children stayed in bed all day to keep warm. When the frost burns outside, hunger is stronger than ever, but Shaindel's larder was empty. She reproached Todie bitterly, wailing, "If you can't feed your wife and children, I will go to the rabbi and get a divorce."

"And what will you do with it, eat it?" Todie retorted.

In the same village there lived a rich man called Lyzer. Because of his stinginess he was known as Lyzer the Miser. He permitted his wife to bake bread only once in four weeks because he had discovered that fresh bread is eaten up more quickly than stale.

Todie had more than once gone to Lyzer for a loan of a few gulden, but Lyzer had always replied: "I sleep better when the money lies in my strongbox rather than in your pocket."

Lyzer had a goat, but he never fed her. The goat had learned to visit the houses of the neighbors, who pitied her and gave her potato peelings. Sometimes, when there were not enough peelings, she would gnaw on the old straw of the thatched roofs. She also had a liking for tree bark. Nevertheless, each year the goat gave birth to a kid. Lyzer milked her but, miser that he was, did not drink the milk himself. Instead he sold it to others.

Todie decided that he would take revenge on Lyzer and at the same time make some much-needed money for himself.

One day, as Lyzer was sitting on a

box eating borscht and dry bread (he used his chairs only on holidays so that the upholstery would not wear out), the door opened and Todie came in.

"Reb Lyzer," he said, "I would like to ask you a favor. My oldest daughter, Basha, is already fifteen and she's about to become engaged. A young man is coming from Janev to look her over. My cutlery is tin, and my wife is ashamed to ask the young man to eat soup with a tin spoon. Would you lend me one of your silver spoons? I give you my holy word that I will return it to you tomorrow."

Lyzer knew that Todie would not dare to break a holy oath and he lent him the spoon.

No young man came to see Basha that evening. As usual, the girl walked around barefoot and in rags, and the silver spoon lay hidden under Todie's shirt. In the early years of his marriage Todie had possessed a set of silver tableware himself. He had, however, long since sold it all, with the exception of three silver teaspoons that were used only on Passover.

The following day, as Lyzer, his feet bare (in order to save his shoes), sat on his box eating borscht and dry bread, Todie returned.

"Here is the spoon I borrowed yesterday," he said, placing it on the table together with one of his own teaspoons.

"What is the teaspoon for?" Lyzer asked.

And Todie said: "Your tablespoon gave birth to a teaspoon. It is her child. Since I am an honest man, I'm returning both mother and child to you."

Lyzer looked at Todie in astonishment. He had never heard of a silver spoon giving birth to another. Nevertheless, his greed overcame his doubt and he happily accepted both spoons. Such an unexpected piece of good fortune! He was overjoyed that he had loaned Todie the spoon.

A few later, as Lyzer (without his coat, to save it) was again sitting on his box eating borscht with dry bread, the door opened and Todie appeared.

"The young man from Janev did not please Basha because he had donkey ears, but this evening another young man is coming to look her over. Shaindel is cooking soup for him, but she's ashamed to serve him with a tin spoon. Would you lend me . . ."

Even before Todie could finish the sentence, Lyzer interrupted. "You want to borrow a silver spoon? Take it with pleasure."

The following day Todie once more returned the spoon and with it one of his own silver teaspoons. He again explained that during the night the large spoon had given birth to a small one and in all good conscience he was bringing back the mother and new-

7

born baby. As for the young man who had come to look Basha over, she hadn't liked him either, because his nose was so long that it reached to his chin. Needless to say that Lyzer the Miser was overjoyed.

Exactly the same thing happened a third time. Todie related that this time his daughter had rejected her suitor because he stammered. He also reported that Lyzer's silver spoon had again given birth to a baby spoon.

"Does it ever happen that a spoon has twins?" Lyzer inquired.

Todie thought it over for a moment. "Why not? I've even heard of a case where a spoon had triplets."

Almost a week passed by and Todie did not go to see Lyzer. But on Friday morning, as Lyzer (in his underdrawers to save his pants) sat on his box eating borscht and dry bread, Todie came in and said, "Good day to you, Reb Lyzer."

"A good morning and many more to you," Lyzer replied in his friendliest manner. "What good fortune brings you here? Did you perhaps come to borrow a silver spoon? If so, help yourself."

"Today I have a very special favor to ask. This evening a young man from the big city of Lublin is coming to look Basha over. He is the son of a rich man and I'm told he is clever and handsome as well. Not only do I need a silver spoon, but since he will remain with us over the Sabbath I need a pair of silver candlesticks, because mine are brass and my wife is ashamed to place them on the Sabbath table. Would you lend me your candlesticks? Immediately after the Sabbath, I will return them to you."

Silver candlesticks are of great value and Lyzer the Miser hesitated, but only for a moment.

Remembering his good fortune with the spoons, he said: "I have eight silver candlesticks in my house. Take them all. I know you will return them to me just as you say. And if it should happen that any of them give birth, I have no doubt that you will be as honest as you have been in the past."

"Certainly," Todie said. "Let's hope for the best."

The silver spoon, Todie hid beneath his shirt as usual. But taking the candlesticks, he went directly to a merchant, sold them for a considerable sum, and brought the money to Shaindel. When Shaindel saw so much money, she demanded to know where he had gotten such a treasure.

"When I went out, a cow flew over

our roof and dropped a dozen silver eggs," Todie replied. "I sold them and here is the money."

"I have never heard of a cow flying over a roof and laying silver eggs," Shaindel said doubtingly.

"There is always a first time," Todie answered. "If you don't want the money, give it back to me."

"There'll be no talk about giving it back," Shaindel said. She knew that her husband was full of cunning and tricks—but when the children are hungry and the larder is empty, it is better not to ask too many questions. Shaindel went to the marketplace and bought meat, fish, white flour, and even some nuts and raisins for a pudding. And since a lot of money still remained, she bought shoes and clothes for the children.

It was a very gay Sabbath in Todie's

house. The boys sang and the girls danced. When the children asked their father where he had gotten the money, he replied: "It is forbidden to mention money during the Sabbath."

Sunday, as Lyzer (barefoot and almost naked to save his clothes) sat on his box finishing up a dry crust of bread with borscht, Todie arrived and, handing him his silver spoon, said: "It's too bad. This time your spoon did not give birth to a baby."

"What about the candlesticks?" Lyzer inquired anxiously.

Todie sighed deeply. "The candlesticks died."

Lyzer got up from his box so hastily that he overturned his plate of borscht.

"You fool!" How can candlesticks die?" he screamed.

"If spoons can give birth, candlesticks can die."

12

Lyzer raised a great hue and cry and had Todie called before the rabbi. When the rabbi heard both sides of the story, he burst out laughing. "It serves you right," he said to Lyzer. "If you hadn't chosen to believe that spoons give birth, now you would not be forced to believe that your candlesticks died."

"But it's all nonsense," Lyzer objected.

"Did you not expect the candlesticks to give birth to other candlesticks?" the rabbi said admonishingly. "If you accept nonsense when it brings you profit, you must also accept nonsense when it brings you loss." And he dismissed the case.

The following day, when Lyzer the Miser's wife brought him his borscht and dry bread, Lyzer said to her, "I will eat only the bread. Borscht is too expensive a food, even without sour cream."

The story of the silver spoons that gave birth and the candlesticks that died spread quickly through the town. All the people enjoyed Todie's victory and Lyzer the Miser's defeat. The shoemaker's and tailor's apprentices, as was their custom whenever there was an important happening, made up a song about it:

Lyzer, put your grief aside.
What if your candlesticks have died?
You're the richest man on earth
With silver spoons that can give birth
And silver eggs as living proof
Of flying cows above your roof.
Don't sit there eating crusts of bread—
To silver grandsons look ahead.

However, time passed and Lyzer's silver spoons never gave birth again.

TSIRTSUR
and
PEZIZA

I n a dark space between the stove
and the wall, where the housewife
stored her brooms, mops, and baking
paddles, there lived an orphan imp
called Peziza. She had only one friend
in the world, Tsirtsur, a cricket. He too
made his home behind the stove in a
crevice between two bricks. An imp
doesn't have to eat at all, but how Tsirtsur managed to survive is a riddle.

Perhaps just the smell of fresh bread baking, a speck of flour that a house breeze swept back there, a drop of moisture in the air were enough for him. In any case, Tsirtsur never complained to Peziza about the lack of food. He dozed all day long. When evening came, he was wide awake and began chirping stories that often continued through the night.

Peziza had never known her father, Lantuch the Imp. Her mother, Pashtida, who came from a wealthy family, had fallen in love with Lantuch. She had often told Peziza about the world that existed beyond the stove and about their relatives, the devils, gnomes, and hobgoblins, each with his own tricks and deviltries. Even so, if one has spent one's entire life behind a stove, one knows little of what is going on in the world, and Peziza had a strong curiosity, a trait no doubt inher-ited from her parents. While Tsirtsur chirped out his endless tales, Peziza dreamed of impish adventures.

Sometimes Peziza would ask Tsir-tsur to tell her how it was outside and he would reply: "My mother said there's only trouble. Cold winds blow, cruel creatures devour each other."

"Nevertheless," Peziza would say thoughtfully, "I'd like to have a look myself at what the devils out there are doing."

And that is exactly what Fate had in mind.

One day there was a loud pounding and hammering. The stove shook, bricks fell. Peziza flew up and down in fright. The houseowners had decided to rebuild the stove. The racket con-tinued all day long and both creatures huddled together until evening. When a piece of wall fell away, Tsirtsur cried, "If we don't get out of here, we'll be killed." There was a break which reached to the outside. They crept through it and found themselves in the back yard of the house. They stood on grass among shrubs and trees. It was the first time Peziza and Tsirtsur had breathed fresh air.

How beautiful the outside was! A huge sky, a moon, stars. Dew was forming. There was the whirring of myriads of crickets. They sounded just like Tsirtsur.

"I will dig myself a hole," Tsirtsur said, "because when the sun rises I must not stay in the open."

"My mother too warned me against the sun," Peziza agreed. "But a hole in the earth is not a proper hiding place for me. There is a hollow in that tree. I will spend the day there."

"The most important thing is that we don't lose each other," Tsirtsur declared. "I'll dig my hole near the roots of your tree."

Tsirtsur immediately began digging. He spoke to Peziza as he worked. "As long as it is summer, the outdoors is not so dangerous. But winter is a bitter time for crickets. It gets cold and something called snow covers the ground. Few crickets survive in such weather."

"Do you mind if I take a look around while you're busy?" Peziza asked.

"You may get lost."

"I won't fly far. I'll recognize this tree. It is taller than the others."

Tsirtsur urged Peziza not to wander away. But curious Peziza was not yet ready to settle down in her hollow. Her desire to see all the new things around her was too strong. She flew off and came to rest on a roof. "I never knew I could fly so well," she thought. Suddenly she heard someone calling to her. She looked in the direction of the voice and saw an imp perched on a weather vane. Although the only other imp Peziza had ever seen was her mother, she knew at once that this imp was a young man. He had two pairs of wings and his horns were transparent. "What is your name?" he asked.

Peziza was so surprised that for a moment she remained speechless. Then she said, "Peziza."

"Peziza? My name is Paziz."

"Is that true or are you joking?"

"Why should I joke? That is my name. Maybe we're related. Let's fly."

Paziz jumped down from the weather vane and somersaulted over the roof to Peziza. He took off and she flew after him, amazed that she was not afraid. The night was full of shadowy creatures. Imps, shades, goblins. One danced on a chimney, another slid down a drainpipe, a third whirled around using a weather vane as a carousel, a fourth clambered up a lamppost. Paziz flew so quickly that it made Peziza dizzy, but she managed to keep up with him. They passed over fields, forests, rivers, lakes, hamlets, and towns. As they flew along, Paziz entertained Peziza with stories of ruined castles, broken windmills, and forsaken houses. How large the world was! How strange the night! How endless the roads! Peziza could have flown on forever, but she knew that when the cock crows and the sun rises, an imp must hide. She also missed Tsirtsur.

"Where are we?" she asked. "I hope I will recognize my tree."

"There is no lack of trees here," Paziz remarked.

"Yes, but my friend Tsirtsur the cricket is waiting for me."

"What kind of a friendship is that? An imp and a cricket?"

"We've always been together. I could never live without him," Peziza replied.

"Very well then. I will bring you back to where we started from."

They had been flying swiftly, but homeward bound they traveled even more quickly than before. In her dreams Peziza had never imagined an imp as clever and brave as Paziz was. He had not spent his life, as she had, in a dark space between a stove and a wall. Each day he found a different resting place. At night he wandered wherever he pleased. He made many friends.

At last the roof where Paziz and Peziza had met came into view and Peziza recognized her tree nearby. To her amazement, when they landed she saw that Tsirtsur was not alone. There was another cricket with him. Tsirtsur too had found a friend and the new cricket was helping him dig his home.

"Where have you been?" Tsirtsur called when he saw Peziza. "I was afraid you were lost."

"I never would have found my way back had it not been for Paziz," she replied and introduced the imp to Tsirtsur.

Tsirtsur cricked politely: "As you see, I too have found a friend. Her name is Grillida."

Fate always has surprises up its sleeve. When Peziza and Tsirtsur were forced to leave their home behind the stove, they were sure their end was

23

near. But the powers that be had their own plans. Instead of misfortune, Peziza found Paziz and Tsirtsur, Grillida. The couples soon became so attached to each other that they were inseparable and before long were married according to the customs of imps and crickets.

As long as summer lasted, they all enjoyed the outdoors. Paziz and Peziza spent their nights flying about and traveled as far as the big city of Lublin. Tsirtsur and Grillida amused themselves by telling each other stories. When day came, the crickets rested in the nest they had dug and the imps slept in their tree hollow.

Little by little the nights began to get cool. A mist rose from the river. The frogs croaked less frequently. One seldom heard the whirring of crickets. Tsirtsur and Grillida kept close together for warmth. Sometimes it rained, lightninged, and thundered at night. Paziz and Peziza did not suffer from the cold, but they, too, had their troubles. First, they felt sorry for their friends, the crickets. Second, the tree in which they lived stood not far from the synagogue and every day they were disturbed by the blowing of the ram's horn. It is known that imps are afraid of the sound of a ram's horn. Whenever Peziza heard the horn's blast, she began to tremble and cry.

One evening Peziza noticed that the chimney leading to the stove behind which she and Tsirtsur used to live had smoke coming out of it. It had been rebuilt and was again in use. All four friends took counsel and decided to try to get behind the stove for the winter. Peziza and Paziz would have no difficulty getting there. They could fly into the house through an open window or through the chimney when the stove was cold. But for Tsirtsur and Grillida it would be a long and difficult journey. However, with the imps helping the crickets along, they all made their way to the old space between the stove and the wall.

The days became shorter, the nights longer. Outdoors it rained and snowed. The frosts came, but behind the stove it was dark, warm, and smelled of bread, cakes, and Sabbath pudding. The owners often toasted noodles and baked apples. In the kitchen, the housewife and her daughters plucked chickens and told stories about ghosts, hobgoblins, and imps. After having spent so much time listening to the people of the house, Peziza and Tsirtsur had learned to understand the language of humans. They had long since discovered that like crickets and imps, humans too dream of love and happiness.

Tsirtsur and Grillida never again left their nest, but Paziz and Peziza would often go out through the chimney to air their wings and revel in the adventures of the netherworld. Each time they returned they brought back new stories for the stay-at-homes. Some were gay and mischievous, others devilish and frightening, but all delighted the crickets and gave Tsirtsur much to chirp about with Grillida in the long winter nights.

UTZEL
and
HIS DAUGHTER
POVERTY

Once there was a man named Utzel. He was very poor and even more lazy. Whenever anyone wanted to give him a job to do, his answer was always the same: "Not today."

"Why not today?" he was asked. And he always replied, "Why not tomorrow?"

Utzel lived in a cottage that had

been built by his great-grandfather.
The thatched roof needed mending
and although the holes let the rain in,
they did not let the smoke from the
stove out. Toadstools grew on the
crooked walls and the floor had rotted
away. There had been a time when
mice lived there, but now there
weren't any because there was nothing
for them to eat. Utzel's wife had
starved to death, but before she died
she had given birth to a baby girl. The
name Utzel gave his daughter was very
fitting. He called her Poverty.

Utzel loved to sleep and each night
he went to bed with the chickens. In
the morning he would complain that
he was tired from so much sleeping
and so he went to sleep again. When
he was not sleeping, he lay on his
broken-down cot, yawning and complaining. He would say to his daughter:

"Other people are lucky. They have money without working. I am cursed."

Utzel was a small man, but as his daughter Poverty grew, she spread out in all directions. She was tall, broad, and heavy. At fifteen she had to lower her head to get through the doorway. Her feet were the size of a man's and puffy with fat. The villagers maintained that the lazier Utzel got, the more Poverty grew.

Utzel loved nobody, was jealous of everybody. He even spoke with envy of cats, dogs, rabbits, and all creatures who didn't have to work for a living. Yes, Utzel hated everybody and everything, but he adored his daughter. He daydreamed that a rich young man would fall in love with her, marry her, and provide for his wife and his father-in-law. But not a young man in the village showed the slightest interest in Poverty. When her father reproached the girl for not making friends and not going out with young men, Poverty would say: "How can I go out in rags and bare feet?"

One day Utzel learned that a certain charitable society in the village loaned poor people money, which they could pay back in small sums over a long period. Lazy as he was, he made a great effort—got up, dressed, and went to the office of the society. "I would like to borrow five gulden," he said to the official in charge.

"What do you intend to do with the money?" he was asked. "We only lend money for useful purposes."

"I want to have a pair of shoes made for my daughter," Utzel explained. "If Poverty has shoes, she will go out with the young people of the village and some wealthy young man will surely fall in love with her. When they get married, I will be able to pay back the five gulden."

The official thought it over. The chances of anyone falling in love with Poverty were very small. Utzel, however, looked so miserable that the official decided to give him the loan. He asked Utzel to sign a promissory note and gave him five gulden.

Utzel had tried to order a pair of shoes for his daughter a few months before. Sandler, the shoemaker, had gone so far as to take Poverty's measurements, but the shoemaker had wanted his money in advance. From the charitable society Utzel went directly to the shoemaker and asked him whether he still had Poverty's measurements.

"And supposing I do?" Sandler replied. "My price is five gulden and I still want my money in advance."

Utzel took out the five gulden and handed them to Sandler. The shoemaker opened a drawer and after some searching brought out the order for Poverty's shoes. He promised to deliver the new shoes in a week, on Friday.

Utzel, who wanted to surprise his daughter, did not tell her about the shoes. The following Friday, as he lay on his cot yawning and complaining, there was a knock on the door and Sandler came in carrying the new shoes. When Poverty saw the shoemaker with a pair of shiny, new shoes in his hand, she cried out in joy. The shoemaker handed her the shoes and told her to try them on. But, alas, she could not get them on her puffy feet. In the months since the measurements

had been taken, Poverty's feet had become even larger than they were before. Now the girl cried out in grief.

Utzel looked on in consternation.
"How is it possible?" he asked. "I

thought her feet stopped growing long ago."

For a while Sandler, too, stood there puzzled. Then he inquired: "Tell me, Utzel, where did you get the five gulden?" Utzel explained that he had borrowed the money from the charitable loan society and had given them a promissory note in return.

"So now you have a debt," exclaimed Sandler. "That makes you even poorer than you were a few months ago. Then you had nothing, but today you have five gulden less than nothing. And since you have grown poorer, Poverty has grown bigger and naturally her feet have grown with her. That is why the shoes don't fit. It is all clear to me now."

"What are we going to do?" Utzel asked in despair.

"There is only one way out for

you," Sandler said. "Go to work. From borrowing one gets poorer and from work one gets richer. When you and your daughter work, she will have shoes that fit."

The idea of working did not appeal to either of them, but it was even worse to have new shoes and go around barefoot. Utzel and Poverty both decided that immediately after the Sabbath they would look for work.

Utzel got a job as a water carrier. Poverty became a maid. For the first time in their lives, they worked diligently. They were kept so busy that they did not even think of the new shoes until one Sabbath morning Poverty decided she'd try them on again. Lo and behold, her feet slipped easily into them. The new shoes fit.

At last Utzel and Poverty understood that all a man possesses he gains through work, and not by lying in bed and being idle. Even animals are industrious. Bees make honey, spiders spin webs, birds build nests, moles dig holes in the earth, squirrels store food for the winter. Before long Utzel got a better job. He rebuilt his house and bought some furniture. Poverty lost more weight. She had new clothes made and dressed prettily like the other girls of the village. Her looks improved too, and a young man began to court her. His name was Mahir and he was the son of a wealthy merchant. Utzel's dream of a rich son-in-law came true, but by then he no longer needed to be taken care of.

Love for his daughter had saved Utzel. In his later years he became so respected he was elected a warden of that same charitable loan society from which he had borrowed five gulden.

On the wall of his office there hung the string with which Sandler had once measured Poverty's feet, and above it the framed motto: "Whatever you can do today, don't put off till tomorrow."

MENASEH'S DREAM

Menaseh was an orphan. He lived with his uncle Mendel, who was a poor glazier and couldn't even manage to feed and clothe his own children. Menaseh had already completed his cheder studies and after the fall holidays was to be apprenticed to a bookbinder.

Menaseh had always been a curious child. He had begun to ask questions as soon as he could talk: "How high is the sky?" "How deep is the earth?" "What is beyond the edge of the world?" "Why are people born?" "Why do they die?"

It was a hot and humid summer day. A golden haze hovered over the village. The sun was as small as a moon and yellow as brass. Dogs loped along with their tails between their legs. Pigeons rested in the middle of the marketplace. Goats sheltered themselves beneath the eaves of the huts, chewing their cuds and shaking their beards.

Menaseh quarreled with his aunt Dvosha and left the house without eating lunch. He was about twelve, with a longish face, black eyes, sunken cheeks. He wore a torn jacket and was barefoot. His only possession was a tattered storybook which he had read scores of times. It was called *Alone in the Wild Forest.* The village in which he lived stood in a forest that surrounded it like a sash and was said to stretch as far as Lublin. It was blueberry time and here and there one might also find wild strawberries. Menaseh made his way through pastures and wheat fields. He was hungry and he tore off a stalk of wheat to chew on the grain. In the meadows, cows were lying down, too hot even to whisk off the flies with their tails. Two horses stood, the head of one near the rump of the other, lost in their horse thoughts. In a field planted in buckwheat the boy was amazed to see a crow perched on the torn hat of a scarecrow.

Once Menaseh entered the forest, it was cooler. The pine trees stood straight as pillars and on their brownish bark hung golden necklaces, the light of the sun shining through the pine needles. The sounds of cuckoo and woodpecker were heard, and an unseen bird kept repeating the same eerie screech.

Menaseh stepped carefully over moss pillows. He crossed a shallow streamlet that purled joyfully over pebbles and stones. The forest was still, and yet full of voices and echoes.

He wandered deeper and deeper into the forest. As a rule, he left stone markers behind, but not today. He was lonely, his head ached and his knees felt weak. "Am I getting sick?" he thought. "Maybe I'm going to die. Then I will soon be with Daddy and Mama." When he came to a blueberry patch, he sat down, picked one berry after another and popped them into his mouth. But they did not satisfy his hunger. Flowers with intoxicating odors grew among the blueberries.

Without realizing it, Menaseh stretched full length on the forest floor. He fell asleep, but in his dream he continued walking.

The trees became even taller, the smells stronger, huge birds flew from branch to branch. The sun was setting. The forest grew thinner and he soon came out on a plain with a broad view of the evening sky. Suddenly a castle appeared in the twilight. Menaseh had never seen such a beautiful structure. Its roof was of silver and from it rose a crystal tower. Its many tall windows were as high as the building itself. Menaseh went up to one of the windows and looked in. On the wall opposite him, he saw his own portrait hanging. He was dressed in luxurious clothes such as he had never owned. The huge room was empty.

"Why is the castle empty?" he won-

dered. "And why is my portrait hanging on the wall?" The boy in the picture seemed to be alive and waiting
impatiently for someone to come.
Then doors opened where there had
been none before, and men and
women came into the room. They
were dressed in white satin and the
women wore jewels and held holiday
prayer books with gold-embossed covers. Menaseh gazed in astonishment.
He recognized his father, his mother,
his grandfathers and grandmothers, and
other relatives. He wanted to rush over
to them, hug and kiss them, but the
window glass stood in his way. He
began to cry. His paternal grandfather,
Tobias the Scribe, separated himself
from the group and came to the window. The old man's beard was as white
as his long coat. He looked both ancient and young. "Why are you cry-

ing?" he asked. Despite the glass that separated them, Menaseh heard him clearly.

"Are you my grandfather Tobias?"

"Yes, my child. I am your grandfather."

"Who does this castle belong to?"

"To all of us."

"To me too?"

"Of course, to the whole family."

"Grandpa, let me in," Menaseh called. "I want to speak to my father and mother."

His grandfather looked at him lovingly and said: "One day you will live with us here, but the time has not yet come."

"How long do I have to wait?"

"That is a secret. It will not be for many, many years."

"Grandpa, I don't want to wait so long. I'm hungry and thirsty and tired.

Please let me in. I miss my father and
mother and you and Grandma. I don't
want to be an orphan."

"My dear child. We know everything. We think about you and we
love you. We are all waiting for the
time when we will be together, but
you must be patient. You have a long
journey to take before you come here
to stay."

"Please, just let me in for a few min-
utes."

Grandfather Tobias left the window
and took counsel with other members
of the family. When he returned, he
said: "You may come in, but only for
a little while. We will show you
around the castle and let you see some
of our treasures, but then you must
leave."

A door opened and Menaseh
stepped inside. He was no sooner over

the threshold than his hunger and wea-
riness left him. He embraced his parents and they kissed and hugged him.
But they didn't utter a word. He felt
strangely light. He floated along and
his family floated with him. His grandfather opened door after door and each
time Menaseh's astonishment grew.

One room was filled with racks of
boys' clothing—pants, jackets, shirts,
coats. Menaseh realized that these were
the clothes he had worn as far back as
he could remember. He also recognized his shoes, socks, caps, and night-
shirts.

A second door opened and he saw
all the toys he had ever owned: the tin
soldiers his father had bought him; the
jumping clown his mother had
brought back from the fair at Lublin;
the whistles and harmonicas; the teddy
bear Grandfather had given him one

Purim and the wooden horse that was the gift of Grandmother Sprintze on his sixth birthday. The notebooks in which he had practiced writing, his pencils and Bible lay on a table. The Bible was open at the title page, with its familiar engraving of Moses holding the holy tablets and Aaron in his priestly robes, both framed by a border of six-winged angels. He noticed his name in the space allowed for it.

Menaseh could hardly overcome his wonder when a third door opened. This room was filled with soap bubbles. They did not burst as soap bubbles do, but floated serenely about, reflecting all the colors of the rainbow. Some of them mirrored castles, gardens, rivers, windmills, and many other sights. Menaseh knew that these were the bubbles he used to blow from his favorite bubble pipe. Now they seemed to have a life of their own.

A fourth door opened. Menaseh entered a room with no one in it, yet it was full of the sounds of happy talk, song, and laughter. Menaseh heard his own voice and the songs he used to sing when he lived at home with his parents. He also heard the voices of his former playmates, some of whom he had long since forgotten.

The fifth door led to a large hall. It was filled with the characters in the stories his parents had told him at bedtime and with the heroes and heroines of *Alone in the Wild Forest*. They were all there: David the Warrior and the Ethiopian princess, whom David saved from captivity; the highwayman Bandurek, who robbed the rich and fed the poor; Velikan the giant, who had one eye in the center of his forehead and who carried a fir tree as a staff in his right hand and a snake in his left; the midget Pitzeles, whose beard dragged on the ground and who was jester to the fearsome King Merodach; and the two-headed wizard Malkizedek, who by witchcraft spirited innocent girls into the desert of Sodom and Gomorrah.

Menaseh barely had time to take them all in when a sixth door opened. Here everything was changing constantly. The walls of the room turned like a carousel. Events flashed by. A golden horse became a blue butterfly; a rose as bright as the sun became a goblet out of which flew fiery grasshoppers, purple fauns, and silver bats. On a glittering throne with seven steps leading up to it sat King Solomon, who somehow resembled Menaseh. He wore a crown and at his feet knelt the Queen of Sheba. A peacock spread his tail and addressed King Solomon in Hebrew. The priestly Levites played their lyres. Giants waved their swords in the air and Ethiopian slaves riding lions served goblets of wine and trays filled with pomegranates. For a moment Menaseh did not understand what it all meant. Then he realized that he was seeing his dreams.

Behind the seventh door, Menaseh glimpsed men and women, animals, and many things that were completely strange to him. The images were not as vivid as they had been in the other rooms. The figures were transparent and surrounded by mist. On the threshold there stood a girl Menaseh's own age. She had long golden braids. Although Menaseh could not see her clearly, he liked her at once. For the first time he turned to his grandfather.

"What is all this?" he asked. And his grandfather replied: "These are the people and events of your future."

"Where am I?" Menaseh asked.

"You are in a castle that has many names. We like to call it the place where nothing is lost. There are many more wonders here, but now it is time for you to leave."

Menaseh wanted to remain in this strange place forever, together with his parents and grandparents. He looked questioningly at his grandfather, who shook his head. Menaseh's parents seemed to want him both to remain and to leave as quickly as possible. They still did not speak, but signaled to him, and Menaseh understood that he was in grave danger. This must be a forbidden place. His parents silently bade him farewell and his face became wet and hot from their kisses. At that moment everything disappeared—the castle, his parents, his grandparents, the girl.

Menaseh shivered and awoke. It was night in the forest. Dew was falling. High above the crowns of the pine trees, the full moon shone and the stars twinkled. Menaseh looked into the face of a girl who was bending over him. She was barefoot and wore a patched skirt; her long braided hair shone golden in the moonlight. She was shaking him and saying: "Get up, get up. It is late and you can't remain here in the forest."

Menaseh sat up. "Who are you?"

"I was looking for berries and I found you here. I've been trying to wake you."

"What is your name?"

"Channeleh. We moved into the village last week."

She looked familiar, but he could not remember meeting her before. Suddenly he knew. She was the girl he had seen in the seventh room, before he woke up.

"You lay there like dead. I was frightened when I saw you. Were you dreaming? Your face was so pale and your lips were moving."

"Yes, I did have a dream."

"What about?"

"A castle."

"What kind of castle?"

Menaseh did not reply and the girl did not repeat her question. She stretched out her hand to him and helped him get up. Together they started toward home. The moon had never seemed so light or the stars so close. They walked with their shadows behind them. Myriads of crickets chirped. Frogs croaked with human voices.

Menaseh knew that his uncle would be angry at him for coming home late. His aunt would scold him for leaving without his lunch. But these things no longer mattered. In his dream he had visited a mysterious world. He had found a friend. Channeleh and he had already decided to go berry picking the next day.

Among the undergrowth and wild mushrooms, little people in red jackets, gold caps, and green boots emerged. They danced in a circle and sang a song which is heard only by those who know that everything lives and nothing in time is ever lost.

WHEN SHLEMIEL
WENT TO WARSAW

Though Shlemiel was a lazybones and a sleepyhead and hated to move, he always daydreamed of taking a trip. He had heard many stories about faraway countries, huge deserts, deep oceans, and high mountains, and often discussed with Mrs. Shlemiel his great wish to go on a long journey. Mrs. Shlemiel would reply: "Long journeys are not for a Shlemiel. You better stay home and mind the children while I go to market to sell my vegetables." Yet Shlemiel could not bring himself to give up his dream of seeing the world and its wonders.

A recent visitor to Chelm had told Shlemiel marvelous things about the city of Warsaw. How beautiful the streets were, how high the buildings and luxurious the stores. Shlemiel decided once and for all that he must see this great city for himself. He knew that one had to prepare for a journey. But what was there for him to take? He had nothing but the old clothes he wore. One morning, after Mrs. Shlemiel left for the market, he told the older boys to stay home from cheder and mind the younger children. Then he took a few slices of bread, an onion, and a clove of garlic, put them in a kerchief, tied it into a bundle, and started for Warsaw on foot.

There was a street in Chelm called Warsaw Street and Shlemiel believed that it led directly to Warsaw. While still in the village, he was stopped by several neighbors who asked him where he was going. Shlemiel told them that he was on his way to Warsaw.

"What will you do in Warsaw?" they asked him.

Shlemiel replied: "What do I do in Chelm? Nothing."

He soon reached the outskirts of town. He walked slowly because the soles of his boots were worn through. Soon the houses and stores gave way to pastures and fields. He passed a peasant driving an ox-drawn plow. After several hours of walking, Shlemiel grew tired. He was so weary that he wasn't even hungry. He lay down on the grass near the roadside for a nap, but before he fell asleep he thought: "When I wake up, I may not remember which is the way to Warsaw and which leads back to Chelm." After pondering a moment, he removed his boots and set them down beside him with the toes pointing toward Warsaw and the heels toward Chelm. He soon fell asleep and dreamed that he was a baker baking onion rolls with poppy seeds. Customers came to buy them and Shlemiel said: "These onion rolls are not for sale."

"Then why do you bake them?"

"They are for my wife, my children, and for me."

Later he dreamed that he was the king of Chelm. Once a year, instead of taxes, each citizen brought him a pot of strawberry jam. Shlemiel sat on a golden throne and nearby sat Mrs. Shlemiel, the queen, and his children, the princes and princesses. They were all eating onion rolls and spooning up big portions of strawberry jam. A carriage arrived and took the royal family to Warsaw, America, and to the River Sambation, which spurts out stones the week long and rests on the Sabbath.

Near the road, a short distance from where Shlemiel slept, was a smithy. The blacksmith happened to come out just in time to see Shlemiel carefully placing his boots at his side with the toes facing in the direction of Warsaw. The blacksmith was a prankster and as soon as Shlemiel was sound asleep he tiptoed over and turned the boots around. When Shlemiel awoke, he felt rested but hungry. He got out a slice of bread, rubbed it with garlic, and took a bite of onion. Then he pulled his boots on and continued on his way.

He walked along and everything looked strangely familiar. He recognized houses that he had seen before. It seemed to him that he knew the people he met. Could it be that he had already reached another town, Shlemiel wondered. And why was it so similar to Chelm? He stopped a passer-by and asked the name of the town. "Chelm," the man replied.

Shlemiel was astonished. How was this possible? He had walked away from Chelm. How could he have arrived back there? He began to rub his forehead and soon found the answer to the riddle. There were two Chelms and he had reached the second one.

Still it seemed very odd that the streets, the houses, the people were so similar to those in the Chelm he had left behind. Shlemiel puzzled over this fact until he suddenly remembered something he had learned in cheder: "The earth is the same everywhere."

And so why shouldn't the second Chelm be exactly like the first one? This discovery gave Shlemiel great satisfaction. He wondered if there was a street here like his street and a house on it like the one he lived in. And indeed he soon arrived at an identical street and house. Evening had fallen. He opened the door and to his amazement saw a second Mrs. Shlemiel with children just like his. Everything was exactly the same as in his own household. Even the cat seemed the same. Mrs. Shlemiel at once began to scold him.

"Shlemiel, where did you go? You left the house alone. And what have you there in that bundle?"

The children all ran to him and cried: "Papa, where have you been?"

Shlemiel paused a moment and then he said: "Mrs. Shlemiel, I'm not your husband. Children, I'm not your papa."

"Have you lost your mind?" Mrs. Shlemiel screamed.

"I am Shlemiel of Chelm One and this is Chelm Two."

Mrs. Shlemiel clapped her hands so hard that the chickens sleeping under the stove awoke in fright and flew out all over the room.

"Children, your father has gone crazy," she wailed. She immediately sent one of the boys for Gimpel, the healer. All the neighbors came crowding in. Shlemiel stood in the middle of the room and proclaimed: "It's true, you all look like the people in my town, but you are not the same. I come from Chelm One and you live in Chelm Two."

"Shlemiel, what's the matter with you?" someone cried. "You're in your own house, with your own wife and children, your own neighbors and friends."

"No, you don't understand. I come from Chelm One. I was on my way to Warsaw, and between Chelm One and Warsaw there is a Chelm Two. And that is where I am."

"What are you talking about. We all know you and you know all of us. Don't you recognize your chickens?"

"No, I'm not in my town," Shlemiel insisted. "But," he continued, "Chelm Two does have the same people and the same houses as Chelm One, and that is why you are mistaken. Tomorrow I will continue on to Warsaw."

"In that case, where is my husband?" Mrs. Shlemiel inquired in a rage, and she proceeded to berate

Shlemiel with all the curses she could think of.

"How should I know where your husband is?" Shlemiel replied.

Some of the neighbors could not help laughing; others pitied the family. Gimpel, the healer, announced that he knew of no remedy for such an illness. After some time, everybody went home.

Mrs. Shlemiel had cooked noodles and beans that evening, a dish that Shlemiel liked especially. She said to him: "You may be mad, but even a madman has to eat."

"Why should you feed a stranger?" Shlemiel asked.

"As a matter of fact, an ox like you should eat straw, not noodles and beans. Sit down and be quiet. Maybe some food and rest will bring you back to your senses."

"Mrs. Shlemiel, you're a good woman. My wife wouldn't feed a stranger. It would seem that there is some small difference between the two Chelms."

The noodles and beans smelled so good that Shlemiel needed no further coaxing. He sat down and as he ate he spoke to the children.

"My dear children, I live in a house that looks exactly like this one. I have a wife and she is as like your mother as two peas are like each other. My children resemble you as drops of water resemble one another."

The younger children laughed; the older ones began to cry. Mrs. Shlemiel said: "As if being a Shlemiel wasn't enough, he had to go crazy in addition. What am I going to do now? I won't be able to leave the children with him when I go to market. Who knows what a madman may do?" She clasped her head in her hands and cried out: "God in heaven, what have I done to deserve this?"

Nevertheless, she made up a fresh bed for Shlemiel; and even though he had napped during the day, near the smithy, the moment his head touched the pillow he fell fast asleep and was soon snoring loudly. He again dreamed that he was the king of Chelm and that his wife, the queen, had fried for him a huge panful of blintzes. Some were filled with cheese, others with blue-berries or cherries, and all were sprin-kled with sugar and cinnamon and were drowning in sour cream. Shle-miel ate twenty blintzes all at once and hid the remainder in his crown for later. In the morning, when Shlemiel awoke, the house was filled with townspeople. Mrs. Shlemiel stood in their midst, her eyes red with weeping. Shlemiel was about to scold his wife for letting so many strangers into the house, but then he remembered that he himself was a stranger here. At home he would have gotten up, washed, and dressed. Now in front of all these people he was at a loss as to what to do. As always when he was embarrassed, he began to scratch his head and pull at his beard. Finally, overcoming his bashfulness, he decided to get up. He threw off the covers and put his bare feet on the floor. "Don't let him run away," Mrs. Shlemiel screamed. "He'll disappear and I'll be a deserted wife, without a Shlemiel."

At this point Baruch, the baker, interrupted. "Let's take him to the Elders. They'll know what to do."

"That's right! Let's take him to the Elders," everybody agreed.

Although Shlemiel insisted that since he lived in Chelm One, the local Elders had no power over him, several of the strong young men helped him into his pants, his boots, his coat and cap and escorted him to the house of Gronam the Ox. The Elders, who had already heard of the matter, had gathered early in the morning to consider what was to be done.

As the crowd came in, one of the Elders, Dopey Lekisch, was saying, "Maybe there really are two Chelms."

"If there are two, then why can't there be three, four, or even a hundred Chelms?" Sender Donkey interrupted.

"And even if there are a hundred Chelms, must there be a Shlemiel in each one of them?" argued Shmendrick Numskull.

Gronam the Ox, the head Elder, listened to all the arguments but was not yet prepared to express an opinion. However, his wrinkled, bulging forehead indicated that he was deep in thought. It was Gronam the Ox who questioned Shlemiel. Shlemiel related everything that had happened to him, and when he finished, Gronam asked: "Do you recognize me?"

"Surely. You are wise Gronam the Ox."

"And in your Chelm is there also a Gronam the Ox?"

"Yes, there is a Gronam the Ox and he looks exactly like you."

"Isn't it possible that you turned around and came back to Chelm?" Gronam inquired.

"Why should I turn around? I'm not a windmill," Shlemiel replied.

"In that case, you are not this Mrs. Shlemiel's husband."

"No, I'm not."

"Then Mrs. Shlemiel's husband, the real Shlemiel, must have left the day you came."

"It would seem so."

"Then he'll probably come back."

"Probably."

"In that case, you must wait until he returns. Then we'll know who is who."

"Dear Elders, my Shlemiel has come back," screamed Mrs. Shlemiel. "I don't need two Shlemiels. One is more than enough."

"Whoever he is, he may not live in your house until everything is made clear," Gronam insisted.

"Where shall I live?" Shlemiel asked.

"In the poorhouse."

"What will I do in the poorhouse?"

"What do you do at home?"

"Good God, who will take care of my children when I go to market?" moaned Mrs. Shlemiel. "Besides, I want a husband. Even a Shlemiel is better than no husband at all."

"Are we to blame that your husband left you and went to Warsaw?" Gronam asked. "Wait until he comes home."

Mrs. Shlemiel wept bitterly and the children cried too. Shlemiel said: "How strange. My own wife always scolded me. My children talked back to me. And here a strange woman and strange children want me to live with them. It looks to me as if Chelm Two is actually better than Chelm One."

"Just a moment. I think I have an idea," interrupted Gronam.

"What is your idea?" Zeinvel Ninny inquired.

"Since we decided to send Shlemiel to the poorhouse, the town will have to hire someone to take care of Mrs. Shlemiel's children so she can go to market. Why not hire Shlemiel for that? It's true, he is not Mrs. Shlemiel's husband or the children's father. But he is so much like the real Shlemiel that the children will feel at home with him."

"What a wonderful idea!" cried Feyvel Thickwit.

"Only King Solomon could have thought of such a wise solution," agreed Treitel the Fool.

"Such a clever way out of this dilemma could only have been thought of in our Chelm," chimed in Shmendrick Numskull.

"How much do you want to be paid

to take care of Mrs. Shlemiel's children?" asked Gronam.

For a moment Shlemiel stood there completely bewildered. Then he said, "Three groschen a day."

"Idiot, moron, ass!" screamed Mrs. Shlemiel. "What are three groschen nowadays? You shouldn't do it for less than six a day." She ran over to Shlemiel and pinched him on the arm. Shlemiel winced and cried out, "She pinches just like my wife."

The Elders held a consultation among themselves. The town budget was very limited. Finally Gronam announced: "Three groschen may be too little, but six groschen a day is definitely too much, especially for a stranger. We will compromise and pay you five groschen a day. Shlemiel, do you accept?"

"Yes, but how long am I to keep this job?"

"Until the real Shlemiel comes home."

Gronam's decision was soon known throughout Chelm and the town admired his great wisdom and that of all the Elders of Chelm.

At first, Shlemiel tried to keep for himself the five groschen that the town paid him. "If I'm not your husband, I don't have to support you," he told Mrs. Shlemiel.

"In that case, since I'm not your wife, I don't have to cook for you, darn your socks, or patch your clothes."

And so, of course, Shlemiel turned over his pay to her. It was the first time that Mrs. Shlemiel had ever gotten any money for the household from Shlemiel. Now when she was in a good mood, she would say to him: "What a pity you didn't decide to go to Warsaw ten years ago."

"Don't you ever miss your husband?" Shlemiel would ask.

"And what about you? Don't you miss your wife?" Mrs. Shlemiel would ask.

And both would admit that they were quite happy with matters as they stood.

Years passed and no Shlemiel returned to Chelm. The Elders had many explanations for this. Zeinvel Ninny believed that Shlemiel had crossed the black mountains and had been eaten alive by the cannibals who live there. Dopey Lekisch thought that Shlemiel most probably had come to the Castle of Asmodeus, where he had been forced to marry a demon princess. Shmendrick Numskull came to the conclusion that Shlemiel had reached the edge of the world and had fallen off. There were many other theories. For example, that the real Shlemiel had lost his memory and had simply forgotten that he was Shlemiel. Such things do happen.

Gronam did not like to impose his theories on other people; however, he was convinced that Shlemiel had gone to the other Chelm, where he had had exactly the same experience as the Shlemiel in this Chelm. He had been hired by the local community and was taking care of the other Mrs. Shlemiel's children for a wage of five groschen a day.

As for Shlemiel himself, he no longer knew what to think. The children were growing up and soon would be able to take care of themselves. Sometimes Shlemiel would sit and ponder. Where is the other Shlemiel? When will he come home? What is my real wife doing? Is she waiting for me, or has she got herself another Shlemiel? These were questions that he could not answer.

Every now and then Shlemiel would still get the desire to go traveling, but he could not bring himself to start out. What was the point of going on a trip if it led nowhere? Often, as he sat alone puzzling over the strange ways of the world, he would become more and more confused and begin humming to himself:

> *"Those who leave Chelm*
> *End up in Chelm.*
> *Those who remain in Chelm*
> *Are certainly in Chelm.*
> *All roads lead to Chelm.*
> *All the world is one big Chelm."*

LEMEL
and
TZIPA

T his story was told me by my
mother, and I'm retelling it here
word for word, as closely as possible.

Once there was a well-to-do coun-
tryman named Tobias, and he and his
wife, Leah, had a daughter, Tzipa, who
was a fool the likes of which you
couldn't find in the entire region.
When Tzipa grew up, marriage bro-
kers began to propose matches for her,

but as soon as a prospective groom came to look her over and she began to spout her nonsense, he would flee from her. It appeared that Tzipa would be left an old maid.

The husband and wife went to ask advice of a rabbi, who told them, "Marriages are made in heaven. Since Tzipa is a fool, heaven will surely provide a foolish groom for her. Just ask around about a youth who's a bigger fool than your daughter, and when the two fools marry, they'll be happy together."

The parents were pleased by this advice. They went to a matchmaker and told him to find the biggest fool in the Lublin province for their daughter. They promised the matchmaker double the fee usually paid for arranging a match. The matchmaker knew that no city contained so many fools as Chelm, so that was where he headed.

He came to a house and saw a youth sitting in front of it and crying. The matchmaker asked, "Young fellow, why are you crying?"

And the youth said, "My mother baked a whole dish of blintzes for Shevuoth. When she went out to buy sour cream for the blintzes, she warned me, 'Lemel, don't eat the blintzes until Shevuoth.' I promised her that I wouldn't, but the moment she left the house I got a great urge for a blintz and I ate one, and after the first I got the urge for another, and a third, and a fourth, and before you know it, I finished the whole dish of blintzes. I was so busy eating blintzes I didn't see the cat watching me. Now I'm very much afraid that when Mother comes back the cat will tell her what I've done and

Mother will pinch me and call me what she calls me anyhow—fool, oaf, dummy, ninny, simp, clod, donkey."

"This Lemel is made for Tzipa," the matchmaker thought.

Aloud he said, "I know how to speak the cat language. I'll tell the cat to say nothing, and when I give a cat an order he listens, for I am the King of the Cats."

Hearing these words, Lemel commenced to dance with joy. The matchmaker began to utter fabricated words to the cat—whatever came to his lips: "Petche-metche-ketche-letche."

Then he asked, "Lemel, do you want a bride?"

"Certainly!"

"I have just the bride for you—no one like her in the whole world. Tzipa is her name."

"Does she have red cheeks?" Lemel

asked. "I like a girl with red cheeks and long braids."

"She has everything you want."

Lemel began to dance anew and clap his hands. At that moment his mother came in with the pot of sour cream. When she saw her son dancing, she asked, "Lemel, what's the big celebration about?"

And Lemel replied, "I ate up all the blintzes and I was afraid the cat would tell, but this man ordered the cat not to talk."

"Dummox! Dolt!" the mother screamed. "What will I do with you? What girl would want to marry such a dunderhead?"

"Mama, I have a bride already!" Lemel exclaimed. "Her name is Tzipa and she has long cheeks and red braids."

A few days later Lemel and Tzipa

drew up their articles of engagement. They could not write their names and Lemel signed with three dots and Tzipa with three dashes. Lemel got a dowry of two hundred gulden. Since Lemel didn't understand about money and didn't know the difference between one banknote and another, Tzipa's father wrapped the five-gulden notes in white paper and the ten-gulden notes in blue paper. Lemel also got a silver watch, but since he couldn't read figures, when he wanted to know the time he stopped a person in the street and asked, "What time is it?" At the same time he added, "I can't see because I've lost my glasses." This was what his mother had told him to use as an excuse.

When the day of the wedding came, Tzipa began to weep bitterly.

Her mother asked, "Tzipa, why are you crying?"

And Tzipa replied, "I'm ashamed to marry a stranger."

The mother said, "I married a stranger too. After the wedding, the husband and wife become close and are no longer strangers."

But Tzipa countered, "You, Mama, married Papa, but I have to marry a complete stranger."

The mother said, "Tzipa, you're a big fool but your groom is a fool too and together you'll be, God willing, two happy fools."

After lengthy discussions, Tzipa allowed herself to be escorted to the wedding canopy.

Some time after the wedding, Tzipa's father said to his son-in-law, "Lemel, your father is a merchant, I'm a merchant, and I want you to be a merchant too. I've given you a dowry. Use it to go into business."

"What's a merchant?" Lemel asked, and his father-in-law said, "A merchant is someone who buys cheap and sells dear. That's how he makes a profit. Take the dowry, go to Lublin, and if you spot a bargain there, buy it as cheaply as possible, then come back here and sell it at a high price."

Lemel did as his father-in-law ordered. Tzipa gave him a chicken wrapped in cabbage leaves for the road. In the wagon, Lemel got hungry and wanted to eat the chicken, but it was raw. Tzipa's mother had told her to give her husband a chicken, but since she didn't say anything about cooking it, Tzipa had given Lemel a raw chicken.

Lemel stopped at an inn. He was very hungry. They asked him what he wanted to eat and he said, "Give me everything you have and I'll eat until I'm full."

Said and done. First they gave him a glass of wine, then another; then an appetizer of tripe with calf's foot. Lemel ate this with lots of bread and horseradish. Then they served him a bowl of noodle soup. After Lemel had finished one bowl of soup, he asked for another. Then they served Lemel a huge portion of meat with groats, cab-

bage, potatoes, and carrots. Lemel finished everything and was still hungry.
Then they served him a compote of
prunes, apples, pears, and raisins.
Lemel gulped it all down and yet his
hunger was still not sated. Finally, they
served him tea with sponge cake and
honey cake. Lemel drank the tea and
ate the cake, but somehow the hunger
still gnawed at him. The innkeeper
said, "I hope that by now you are full."

But Lemel replied, "No, I'm still
hungry."

The innkeeper took a cookie out of
the cabinet and said, "Try this."

Lemel ate the cookie and immediately felt sated. He said, "Now I'm full.
Had I known that you can get full
from a cookie, I needn't have ordered
all those other dishes."

The innkeeper promptly saw that he
was dealing with a dolt. He himself was

a swindler and he said, "Now it's too late. But if you ever come here again, I'll give you such a cookie right off the bat and you won't have to order the other dishes. Now, be so good as to pay for the meal."

Lemel took from his purse the banknotes rolled in white paper and those rolled in blue paper and he said, "One paper contains the five-gulden bills and the other the ten-gulden bills, but I don't remember which is which."

The innkeeper unrolled the two stacks, and as befits a swindler, he told Lemel that a ten-gulden was a five-gulden bill. He also swindled Lemel with the change.

In Lublin Lemel went from store to store seeking bargains, but somehow there were no bargains to be found. Lying in bed at night, Lemel began to think about the miraculous cookie which made you instantly full. "If I knew how to bake such cookies I'd be rich," Lemel said to himself. "There isn't enough food in Chelm, the people are hungry, and everyone would welcome such cookies."

He himself had felt sated for nearly twenty hours after eating this cookie.

The next day Lemel headed home and he stopped at the same inn. He ordered the miraculous cookie, but the innkeeper said, "I just now served the last of them to a guest. But I can sell you the recipe. Believe me, when you bake these cookies in Chelm you'll sell them for a big profit and you'll become as rich as Rothschild."

"What does this recipe cost?"

The innkeeper named a high price, but Lemel decided that by baking such cookies he could get back all the money he would pay, with a huge

profit besides. So he bought the recipe.
Having already seen that Lemel
couldn't read, write, or even deter-
mine the value of a coin, the innkeeper
composed the following recipe:

Take three quarters of duck's milk,
five pounds of flour ground from
iron, two pounds of cheese made
from snow, one pound of fat from a
flintstone, a half pound of feathers
from a red crow, and a quarter pound
of juice squeezed from copper.
Throw it all in a pot made of wax and
let it cook three days and three nights
over the fire of a potato tree. After
three days, knead a dough out of the
mixture, cut out the cookies with a
knife made of butter, and bake them
in an oven made of ice till they turn
red, brown, and yellow. Then dig a
pit, throw in the whole mess, and put
up a board with a sign over it reading:

WHEN YOU SEND A FOOL TO MARKET,
THE MERCHANTS REJOICE.

After Lemel finished paying for the
meal and the recipe, he barely had
enough left for the fare home. But he
was pleased with the bargain he had
made.

When he came home and told
Tzipa about the miraculous cookie,
she began to clap her hands and dance.
But the joy didn't last long. When
Lemel's father-in-law came home and
read the recipe, he became furious and
screamed, "Lemel, you've been swindled!"

Tzipa promptly began to cry. Tzipa's mother cried along with her.

After a while, Lemel said, "All my
troubles stem from the fact that I can't
read. I must learn to read, and the
quicker the better."

"Yes, my son," Tzipa's father said. "A merchant must be able to read and write."

Since there were no teachers in the village, Lemel resolved to go to Lublin to learn to read. Again, the father-in-law gave him money for the fare and to pay for the lessons. In Lublin, Lemel went to Lewartow Street to seek out a teacher. He walked past a store displaying eyeglasses in the window. He looked inside and saw a customer put on a pair of glasses and glance into a book while the proprietor asked, "Now can you read?"

"Yes, now I can read well," the customer said.

Lemel thought to himself, "Since putting on glasses enables you to read, what do I need with a teacher?"

Lemel had no urge to study. He yearned to go home to Tzipa.

He went into the store and said to

the proprietor, "Give me a pair of glasses so that I can read."

The proprietor asked what strength glasses he had worn before and Lemel said, "I don't know anything about it. Let me test them."

The proprietor handed him a pair of glasses and opened a book before him.

Lemel looked into the book and said, "I can't read."

"I'll give you stronger glasses," the proprietor said.

Lemel tested the second pair and said, "I still can't read."

The proprietor offered him many different glasses to try but Lemel kept giving the same answer—he still couldn't read.

After a while, the proprietor said, "Forgive me, but maybe you can't read at all?"

"If I could read, I wouldn't have

come to you in the first place," Lemel said.

"In that case, you must first go to a teacher and learn to read. You can't learn to read from putting on a pair of glasses," the storekeeper said.

Lemel grew depressed by the answer. He had been prepared to put on the glasses and go back home. After a while Lemel decided that he couldn't go on without Tzipa. He missed her terribly. He went to seek out a teacher not so much to learn how to read as to have the teacher write a letter home for him. He soon found one. When Lemel asked how long it would take for him to learn to read, the teacher said, "It could take a year, but not less than a half year."

Lemel grew very sad. He said to the teacher, "Could you write a letter for me? I want to send a letter to my Tzipa."

"Yes, I could write a letter for you. Tell me what to write."

Lemel began to dictate:

Dear Tzipa,

I'm already in Lublin. I thought that if you put on glasses you could read, but the proprietor of the store said that glasses don't help. The teacher says it would take a half year or a whole year to teach me to read and that I would have to stay here in Lublin the whole time. Dear Tzipele, I love you so much that when I'm away from you one day I must die of longing. If I am without you for a half year, I'll have to die maybe a hundred times or even more. Therefore, I've decided to come home, if my father-in-law, your father, will agree. I hope to find some kind of work for which you don't have to read or write.

Longingly,
Your Lemel

When Tzipa received this letter and her father read it to her, she burst into tears and dictated a letter to Lemel which read as follows:

Dear Lemel,

When you don't see me for a day you must die, but when I don't see you for a minute, I go crazy. Yes, my dear Lemel, come back. I don't need a writer but a good husband and, later, a houseful of children—six boys and six girls. Father will find some kind of work for you. Don't wait but come straight home, because if you come back dead and find me crazy, it wouldn't be so good for either of us.

Your devoted Tzipa

When the teacher read Tzipa's letter to Lemel he burst out crying. That very same day he started for home. Before getting into the wagon in Lublin, he went to the market to buy a present for Tzipa. He went into a mirror store with the intention of buying her a mirror. At the same time he told the storekeeper everything that had happened to him—how he had been swindled with the cookie and how he had been unable to learn to read with the glasses.

The storekeeper was a prankster and dishonest as well. He said: "Such people as you, Lemel, and your wife, Tzipa, should be many. I have a potion which when you drink it will make you become double, triple, quadruple. How would you like there to be ten Lemels and ten Tzipas who would all love each other? One Lemel and one Tzipa could stay home all day, another set could go to market to buy goods, a third set could take a walk, a fourth set could eat blintzes with sour cream, and the fifth set could go to Lublin and learn to read and write."

"How is this possible?" Lemel asked.

"Drink the potion and you'll see for yourself."

The storekeeper gave Lemel a glass of plain water and told him to drink merely one drop of it. Then he led Lemel into a room where two mirrors hung facing each other, one of which was tilted slightly to the side. When Lemel came into the room he saw not one Lemel in the mirror but a whole row of Lemels. He walked over to the other mirror and there were many Lemels there too.

The storekeeper stood by the door and said, "Well, did I deceive you?"

"Oh, I can't believe my own eyes!" Lemel exclaimed. "How much is this potion?"

"It's very expensive," the store-keeper said, "but for you, I'll make it cheap. Give me all the money you have except for your fare home. You've snagged a terrific bargain."

Lemel paid on the spot and the storekeeper gave him a big bottle filled with water. He told him, "You and your Tzipa need drink only one drop a day. This bottle will last you for years. If it gets used up, you can always come back to Lublin and I'll refill it for you for free. Wait, I'll give you a written guarantee."

The storekeeper took out a sheet of paper and wrote on it: "God loves fools. That's why He made so many of them."

When Lemel came home and his father-in-law saw the bottle of water and read the note, he realized that Lemel had been swindled again.

But when Lemel saw Tzipa his joy was so intense he forgot all his troubles. He kissed and hugged her and cried, "I don't need many Tzipas. One Tzipa is enough for me, even if I should live to be a thousand!"

"And I don't need many Lemels. One Lemel is enough for me, even if I should live to be a million!" Tzipa exclaimed.

Yes, Lemel and Tzipa were both fools, but they possessed more love than all the sages. After a while, Lemel bought a horse and wagon and became a coachman. For this he didn't have to know how to read or write. He drove passengers to and from Chelm and everyone liked him for his punctuality, his friendliness, and for the love he showed his horse. Tzipa began to have children and bore Lemel six boys and six girls. The boys took after Tzipa and the girls after Lemel, but they were all good-natured fools and they all found mates in Chelm. Lemel and Tzipa lived happily to a ripe old age, long enough to enjoy a whole tribe of grandchildren, great-grandchildren, and great-great-grandchildren.

THE CAT WHO THOUGHT SHE WAS A DOG
and
THE DOG WHO THOUGHT HE WAS A CAT

Once there was a poor peasant, Jan Skiba by name. He lived with his wife and three daughters in a one-room hut with a straw roof, far from the village. The house had a bed, a bench bed, and a stove, but no mirror. A mirror was a luxury for a poor peasant. And why would a peasant need a mirror? Peasants aren't curious about their appearance.

But this peasant did have a dog and a cat in his hut. The dog was named Burek and the cat Kot. They had both been born within the same week. As little food as the peasant had for himself and his family, he still wouldn't let his dog and cat go hungry. Since the dog had never seen another dog and the cat had never seen another cat and they saw only each other, the dog thought he was a cat and the cat thought she was a dog. True, they were far from being alike by nature. The dog barked and the cat meowed. The dog chased rabbits and the cat lurked after mice. But must all creatures be exactly like their own kind? The peasant's children weren't exactly alike either. Burek and Kot lived on good terms, often ate from the same dish, and tried to mimic each other. When Burek barked, Kot tried to bark along, and when Kot meowed, Burek tried to meow too. Kot occasionally chased rabbits and Burek made an effort to catch a mouse.

The peddlers who bought groats, chickens, eggs, honey, calves, and whatever was available from the peasants in the village never came to Jan Skiba's poor hut. They knew that Jan was so poor he had nothing to sell. But one day a peddler happened to stray there. When he came inside and began to lay out his wares, Jan Skiba's wife and daughters were bedazzled by all the pretty doodads. From his sack the peddler drew yellow beads, false pearls, tin earrings, rings, brooches, colored kerchiefs, garters, and other such trinkets. But what enthralled the women of the house most was a mirror set in a wooden frame. They asked the peddler its price and he said a half gulden, which was a lot of money for poor peasants. After a while, Jan Skiba's wife, Marianna, made a proposition to the peddler. She would pay him five groshen a month for the mirror. The peddler hesitated a moment. The mirror took up too much space in his sack and there was always the danger it might break. He, therefore, decided to go along, took the first payment of five groshen from Marianna, and left the mirror with the family. He visited the region often and he knew the Skibas to be honest people. He would gradually get his money back and a profit besides.

The mirror created a commotion in the hut. Until then Marianna and the children had seldom seen themselves. Before they had the mirror, they had only seen their reflections in the barrel of water that stood by the door. Now they could see themselves clearly and they began to find defects in their faces, defects they had never noticed before. Marianna was pretty but she had a tooth missing in front and she felt that this made her ugly. One daughter discovered that her nose was too snub and too broad; a second that her chin was too narrow and too long; a third that her face was sprinkled with freckles. Jan Skiba too caught a glimpse of himself in the mirror and grew displeased by his thick lips and his teeth, which protruded like a buck's. That day, the women of the house became so absorbed in the mirror they didn't cook supper, didn't make up the bed, and neglected all the other household tasks. Marianna had heard of a dentist in the big city who could replace a missing tooth, but such things were expensive. The girls tried to console each other that they were pretty

THE CAT AND THE DOG

enough and that they would find suitors, but they no longer felt as jolly as before. They had been afflicted with the vanity of city girls. The one with the broad nose kept trying to pinch it together with her fingers to make it narrower; the one with the too-long chin pushed it up with her fist to make it shorter; the one with the freckles wondered if there was a salve in the city that could remove freckles. But where would the money come from for the fare to the city? And what about the money to buy this salve? For the first time the Skiba family deeply felt its poverty and envied the rich.

But the human members of the household were not the only ones affected. The dog and the cat also grew disturbed by the mirror. The hut was low and the mirror had been hung just above a bench. The first time the cat sprang up on the bench and saw her image in the mirror, she became terribly perplexed. She had never before seen such a creature. Kot's whiskers bristled, she began to mcow at her reflection and raised a paw to it, but the other creature meowed back and raised her paw too. Soon the dog jumped up on the bench, and when he saw the other dog he became wild with rage and shock. He barked at the other dog and showed him his teeth, but the other barked back and bared his fangs too. So great was the distress of Burek and Kot that for the first time in their lives they turned on each other. Burek took a bite out of Kot's throat and Kot hissed and spat at him and clawed his muzzle. They both started to bleed and the sight of blood aroused them so that they nearly killed or crippled each other. The members of the household

barely managed to separate them. Because a dog is stronger than a cat,
Burek had to be tied outside, and he
howled all day and all night. In their
anguish, both the dog and the cat
stopped eating.

When Jan Skiba saw the disruption

the mirror had created in his household, he decided a mirror wasn't what his family needed. "Why look at yourself," he said, "when you can see and admire the sky, the sun, the moon, the stars, and the earth, with all its forests, meadows, rivers, and plants?" He took the mirror down from the wall and put it away in the woodshed. When the peddler came for his monthly installment, Jan Skiba gave him back the mirror and in its stead, bought kerchiefs and slippers for the women. After the mirror disappeared, Burek and Kot returned to normal. Again Burek thought he was a cat and Kot was sure she was a dog. Despite all the defects the girls had found in themselves, they made good marriages. The village priest heard what had happened at Jan Skiba's house and he said, "A glass mirror shows only the skin of the body. The real image of a person is in his willingness to help himself and his family and, as far as possible, all those he comes in contact with. This kind of mirror reveals the very soul of the person."

NAFTALI THE
STORYTELLER
and
HIS HORSE, SUS

I

The father, Zelig, and the mother, Bryna, both complained that their son, Naftali, loved stories too much. He could never go to sleep unless his mother first told him a story. At times she had to tell him two or three stories before he would close his eyes.

He always demanded: "Mama, more, more! . . ."

Fortunately, Bryna had heard many stories from her mother and grandmother. Zelig himself, a coachman, had many things to tell—about spirits who posed as passengers and imps who stole into stables at night and wove braids into the horses' tails and elflocks into their manes. The nicest story was about when Zelig had still been a young coachman.

One summer night Zelig was coming home from Lublin with an empty wagon. It just so happened that he hadn't picked up any passengers from Lublin to his hometown, Janów. He drove along a road that ran through a forest. There was a full moon. It cast silvery nets over the pine branches and strings of pearls over the bark of the tree trunks. Night birds cried. From time to time a wolf's howl was heard. In those days the Polish woods still swarmed with bears, wolves, foxes, martens, and many other wild beasts. That night Zelig was despondent. When his wagon was empty of passengers, his wallet was empty of money, and there wouldn't be enough for Bryna to prepare for the Sabbath.

Suddenly Zelig saw lying in the road a sack that appeared to be full of flour or ground sugar. Zelig stopped his horse and got down to take a look. A sack of flour or sugar would come in handy in a household.

Zelig untied the sack, opened it, took a lick, and decided that it was ground sugar. He lifted the sack, which was unusually heavy. Zelig was accustomed to carrying his passengers' baggage and he wondered why a sack of sugar should feel so heavy.

"It seems I didn't have enough to eat at the inn," Zelig thought. "And when you don't eat enough, you lose your strength."

He loaded the sack into the wagon. It was so heavy that he nearly strained himself.

He sat down on the driver's box and pulled on the reins, but the horse didn't move.

Zelig tugged harder and cried out, *"Wyszta!"* which in Polish means "Giddap!"

But even though the horse pulled with all his might, the wagon still wouldn't move forward.

"What's going on here?" Zelig wondered. "Can the sack be so heavy that the horse cannot pull it?"

This made no sense, for the horse had often drawn a wagonful of passengers along with their baggage.

"There is something here that's not as it should be," Zelig said to himself. He got down again, untied the sack, and took another lick. God in heaven, the sack was full of salt, not sugar!

Zelig stood there dumbfounded. How could he have made such a mistake? He licked again, and again, and it was salt.

"Well, it's one of those nights!" Zelig mumbled to himself.

He decided to heave the sack off the wagon, since it was clear that evil spirits were toying with him. But by now the sack had become as heavy as if it were filled with lead. The horse turned his head backward and stared, as if curious as to what was going on.

Suddenly Zelig heard laughter coming from inside the sack. Soon afterward the sack crumbled and out popped a creature with the eyes of a calf, the horns of a goat, and the wings of a bat. The creature said in a human voice, "You didn't lick sugar or salt but an imp's tail."

And with these words the imp burst into wild laughter and flew away.

Dozens of times Zelig the coachman told this same story to Naftali but Naftali never grew tired of hearing it. He

could picture it all—the forest, the
night, the silver moon, the curious eye
of the horse, the imp. Naftali asked all
kinds of questions: Did the imp have a
beard? Did it have feet? How did its
tail look? Where did it fly off to?

Zelig couldn't answer all the questions. He had been too frightened at the
time to notice the details. But to the last
question Zelig replied, "He probably
flew to beyond the Dark Regions,
where people don't go and cattle don't
stray, where the sky is copper, the earth
iron, and where the evil forces live
under roofs of petrified toadstools and in
tunnels abandoned by moles."

II

Like all the children in town, Naftali
rose early to go to cheder. He studied

more diligently than the other children. Why? Because Naftali was eager to learn to read. He had seen older boys reading storybooks and he had been envious of them. How happy was one who could read a story from a book!

At six, Naftali was already able to read a book in Yiddish, and from then on he read every storybook he could get his hands on. Twice a year a bookseller named Reb Zebulun visited Janów, and among the other books in the sack he carried over his shoulder were some storybooks. They cost two groshen a copy, and although Naftali got only two groshen a week allowance from his father, he saved up enough to buy a number of storybooks each season. He also read the stories in his mother's Yiddish Pentateuch and in her books of morals.

When Naftali grew older, his father began to teach him how to handle horses. It was the custom in those days for a son to take over his father's livelihood. Naftali loved horses very much but he wasn't anxious to become a coachman driving passengers from Janów to Lublin and from Lublin to Janów. He wanted to become a bookseller with a sackful of storybooks.

His mother said to him, "What's so good about being a bookseller? From toting the sack day in day out, your back becomes bent, and from all the walking, your legs swell."

Naftali knew that his mother was right and he thought a lot about what he would do when he grew up. Suddenly he came up with a plan that seemed to him both wise and simple. He would get himself a horse and wagon, and instead of carrying the books on his back, he would carry them in the wagon.

His father, Zelig, said, "A bookseller doesn't make enough to support himself, his family, and a horse besides."

"For me it will be enough."

One time when Reb Zebulun the bookseller came to town, Naftali had a talk with him. He asked him where he got the storybooks and who wrote them. The bookseller told him that in Lublin there was a printer who printed these books, and in Warsaw and Vilna there were writers who wrote them. Reb Zebulun said that he could sell many more storybooks, but he lacked the strength to walk to all the towns and villages, and it didn't pay him to do so.

Reb Zebulun said, "I'm liable to come to a town where there are only two or three children who want to read storybooks. It doesn't pay me to walk there for the few groshen I might earn nor does it pay me to keep a horse or hire a wagon."

"What do these children do without storybooks?" Naftali asked. And Reb Zebulun replied, "They have to make do. Storybooks aren't bread. You can live without them."

"I couldn't live without them," Naftali said.

During this conversation Naftali also asked where the writers got all those stories and Reb Zebulun said, "First of all, many unusual things happen in the world. A day doesn't go by without some rare event happening. Besides, there are writers who make up such stories."

"They make them up?" Naftali asked in amazement. "If that is so, then they are liars."

"They are not liars," Reb Zebulun replied. "The human brain really can't make up a thing. At times I read a story that seems to me completely unbelievable, but I come to some place and I hear that such a thing actually happened. The brain is created by God, and human thoughts and fantasies are also God's works. Even dreams come from God. If a thing doesn't happen today, it might easily happen tomorrow. If not in one country, then in another. There are endless worlds and what doesn't happen on earth can happen in another world. Whoever has eyes that see and ears that hear absorbs enough stories to last a lifetime and to tell to his children and grandchildren."

That's what old Reb Zebulun said, and Naftali listened to his words agape.

Finally, Naftali said, "When I grow up, I'll travel to all the cities, towns, and villages, and I'll sell storybooks everywhere, whether it pays me or not."

Naftali had decided on something else too—to become a writer of storybooks. He knew full well that for this you had to study, and with all his heart he determined to learn. He also began to listen more closely to what people said, to what stories they told, and to how they told them. Each person had his or her own manner of speaking. Reb Zebulun told Naftali, "When a day passes, it is no longer there. What remains of it? Nothing more than a story. If stories weren't told or books weren't written, man would live like the beasts, only for the day."

Reb Zebulun said, "Today we live, but by tomorrow today will be a story. The whole world, all human life, is one long story."

III

Ten years went by. Naftali was now a young man. He grew up tall, slim, fair-skinned, with black hair and blue eyes. He had learned a lot at the studyhouse and in the yeshiva and he was also an expert horseman. Zelig's mare had borne a colt and Naftali pastured and raised it. He called him Sus. Sus was a playful colt. In the summer he liked to roll in the grass. He whinnied like the tinkling sound of a bell. Sometimes, when Naftali washed and curried him and tickled his neck, Sus burst out in a sound that resembled laughter. Naftali rode him bareback like a Cossack. When Naftali passed the marketplace astride Sus, the town girls ran to the windows to look out.

After a while Naftali built himself a wagon. He ordered the wheels from

Leib the blacksmith. Naftali loaded the wagon with all the storybooks he had collected during the years and he rode with his horse and his goods to the nearby towns. Naftali bought a whip, but he swore solemnly to himself that he would never use it. Sus didn't need to be whipped or even to have the whip waved at him. He pulled the light wagonful of books eagerly and easily. Naftali seldom sat on the box but walked alongside his horse and told him stories. Sus cocked his ears when Naftali spoke to him and Naftali was sure that Sus understood him. At times, when Naftali asked Sus whether he had liked a story, Sus whinnied, stomped his foot on the ground, or licked Naftali's ear with his tongue as if he meant to say, "Yes, I understand. . . ."

Reb Zebulun had told him that animals live only for the day, but Naftali was convinced that animals have a memory too. Sus often remembered the road better than he, Naftali, did. Naftali had heard the story of a dog whose masters had lost him on a distant journey and months after they had come home without their beloved pet, he showed up. The dog crossed half of Poland to come back to his owners. Naftali had heard a similar story about a cat. The fact that pigeons fly back to their coops from very far away was known throughout the world. In those days, they were often used to deliver letters. Some people said this was memory, others called it instinct. But what did it matter what it was called? Animals didn't live for the day only.

Naftali rode from town to town; he often stopped in villages and sold his storybooks. The children everywhere loved Naftali and his horse, Sus. They brought all kinds of good things from home for Sus—potato peels, turnips, and pieces of sugar—and each time Sus got something to eat he waved his tail and shook his head, which meant "Thank you."

Not all the children were able to study and learn to read, and Naftali would gather a number of young children, seat them in the wagon, and tell them a story, sometimes a real one and sometimes a made-up one.

Wherever he went, Naftali heard all kinds of tales—of demons, hobgoblins, windmills, giants, dwarfs, kings, princes, and princesses. He would tell a story nicely, with all the details, and the children never grew tired of listening to him. Even grownups came to listen. Often the grownups invited Naftali home for a meal or a place to sleep. They also liked to feed Sus.

When a person does his work not only for money but out of love, he brings out the love in others. When a child couldn't afford a book, Naftali

gave it to him free. Soon Naftali became well known throughout the region. Eventually, he came to Lublin.

In Lublin, Naftali heard many aston-
ishing stories. He met a giant seven feet
tall who traveled with a circus and a
troupe of midgets. At the circus Naftali
saw horses who danced to music, as
well as dancing bears. One trickster
swallowed a knife and spat it out again,
another did a somersault on a high
wire, a third flew in the air from one
trapeze to another. A girl stood on a
horse's back while it raced round and
round the circus ring. Naftali struck up
an easy friendship with the circus people and he listened to their many inter-
esting stories. They told of fakirs in
India who could walk barefoot over
burning coals. Others let themselves be
buried alive, and after they were dug
out several days later, they were

healthy and well. Naftali heard astounding stories about sorcerers and miracle workers who could read minds and predict the future. He met an old man who had walked from Lublin to the Land of Israel, then back again. The old man told Naftali about cabalists who lived in caves behind Jerusalem, fasted from one Sabbath to the next, and learned the secrets of God, the angels, the seraphim, the cherubim, and the holy beasts.

The world was full of wonders and Naftali had the urge to write them down and spread them far and wide over all the cities, towns, and villages.

In Lublin, Naftali went to the bookstores and bought storybooks, but he soon saw that there weren't enough storybooks to be had. The storekeepers said that it didn't pay the printers to print them since they brought in so little money. But could everything be measured by money? There were children and even grownups everywhere who yearned to hear stories and Naftali decided to tell all that he had heard. He himself hungered for stories and could never get enough of them.

IV

More years passed. Naftali's parents were no longer living. Many girls had fallen in love with Naftali and wanted to marry him, but he knew that from telling stories and selling storybooks he could not support a family. Besides, he had become used to wandering. How many stories could he hear or tell living in one town? He therefore decided to stay on the road. Horses normally live some twenty-odd years, but Sus was one of those rare horses who live a long time. However, no one lives forever. At forty Sus began to show signs of old age. He seldom galloped now, nor were his eyes as good as they once were. Naftali was already gray himself and the children called him Grandpa.

One time Naftali was told that on the road between Lublin and Warsaw lay an estate where all booksellers came, since the owner was very fond of reading and hearing stories. Naftali asked the way and he was given directions to get there. One spring day he came to the estate. Everything that had been said turned out to be true. The owner of the estate, Reb Falik, gave him a warm welcome and bought many books from him. The children in the nearby town had already heard about Naftali the storyteller and they

snatched up all the storybooks he had
brought with him. Reb Falik had
many horses grazing and when they
saw Sus they accepted him as one of
their own. Sus promptly began to
chew the grass where many yellow
flowers grew and Naftali told Reb
Falik one story after another. The
weather was warm, birds sang, twit-
tered, and trilled; each in its own
voice.

The estate contained a tract of forest
where old oaks grew. Some of the oaks
were so thick they had to be hundreds
of years old. Naftali was particularly
taken by one oak standing in the center of a meadow. It was the thickest
oak Naftali had ever seen in his life. Its
roots were spread over a wide area and
you could tell that they ran deep. The
crown of the oak spread far and wide,
and it cast a huge shadow. When Naf-

tali saw this giant oak, which had to be older than all the oaks in the region, it occurred to him: "What a shame an oak hasn't a mouth to tell stories with!"

This oak had lived through many generations. It may have gone back to the times when idol worshippers still lived in Poland. It surely knew the time when the Jews had come to Poland from the German states where they had been persecuted and the Polish king, Kazimierz I, had opened the gates of the land to them. Naftali suddenly realized that he was tired of wandering. He now envied the oak for standing so long in one place, deeply rooted in God's earth. For the first time in his life Naftali got the urge to settle down in one place. He also thought of his horse. Sus was undoubtedly tired of trekking over the roads. It would do him good to get some rest in the few years left him.

Just as Naftali stood there thinking these thoughts, the owner of the estate, Reb Falik, came along in a buggy. He stopped the buggy near Naftali and said, "I see you're completely lost in thought. Tell me what you're thinking."

At first Naftali wanted to tell Reb Falik that many kinds of foolish notions ran through the human mind and that not all of them could be described. But after a while he thought, "Why not tell him the truth?"

Reb Falik seemed a good-hearted man. He had a silver-white beard and eyes that expressed the wisdom and goodness that sometimes come with age. Naftali said, "If you have the patience, I'll tell you."

"Yes, I have the patience. Take a

seat in the buggy. I'm going for a drive and I want to hear what a man who is famous for his storytelling thinks about."

Naftali sat down in the buggy. The horses hitched to the buggy walked slowly and Naftali told Reb Falik the story of his life, as well as what his thoughts were when he saw the giant oak. He told him everything, kept nothing back.

When Naftali finished, Reb Falik said, "My dear Naftali, I can easily fulfill all your wishes and fantasies. I am, as you know, an old man. My wife died some time ago. My children live in the big cities. I love to hear stories and I also have lots of stories to tell. If you like, I'll let you build a house in the shade of the oak and you can stay there as long as I live and as long as you live. I'll have a stable built for your horse near the house and you'll both live out your lives in peace. Yes, you are right. You cannot wander forever. There comes a time when every person wants to settle in one place and drink in all the charms that the place has to offer."

When Naftali heard these words, a great joy came over him. He thanked Reb Falik again and again, but Reb Falik said, "You need not thank me so much. I have many peasants and servants here, but I don't have a single person I can talk to. We'll be friends and we'll teach each other lots of stories. What's life, after all? The future isn't here yet and you cannot foresee what it will bring. The present is only a moment and the past is one long story. Those who don't tell stories and don't hear stories live only for that moment, and that isn't enough."

V

Reb Falik's promise wasn't merely words. The very next day he ordered his people to build a house for Naftali the storyteller. There was no shortage of lumber or of craftsmen on the estate. When Naftali saw the plans for the house, he grew disturbed. He needed only a small house for himself and a stable for Sus. But the plans called for a big house with many rooms. Naftali asked Reb Falik why such a big house was being built for him, and Reb Falik replied, "You will need it."

"What for?" Naftali asked.

Gradually, the secret came out. During his lifetime Reb Falik had accumulated many books, so many that he couldn't find room for them in his own big house and many books had to be stored in the cellar and in the attic.

Besides, in his talks with Reb Falik, Naftali had said that he had many of his own stories and stories told him by others written down on paper and that he had collected a chestful of manuscripts, but he hadn't been able to have these stories printed, for the printers in Lublin and in the other big cities demanded a lot of money to print them and the number of buyers of storybooks in Poland wasn't large enough to cover such expenses.

Alongside Naftali's house, Reb Falik had a print shop built. He ordered crates of type from Lublin (in those days there was no such thing as a typesetting machine) as well as a hand press. From now on Naftali would have the opportunity to set and print his own storybooks. When he learned what Reb Falik was doing for him, Naftali couldn't believe his ears. He said, "Of all the stories I have ever heard or told, for me this will be by far the nicest."

That very summer everything was ready—the house, the library, the print shop. Winter came early. Right after Succoth the rains began, followed by snow. In winter there is little to do on an estate. The peasants sat in their huts and warmed themselves by their stoves or they went to the tavern. Reb Falik and Naftali spent lots of time together. Reb Falik himself was a treasure trove of stories. He had met many famous squires. In his time he had visited the fairs in Danzig, Leipzig, and Amsterdam. He had even made a trip to the Holy Land and had seen the Western Wall, the Cave of Machpelah, and Rachel's Tomb. Reb Falik told many tales and Naftali wrote them down.

Sus's stable was too big for one

horse. Reb Falik had a number of old horses on his estate that could no longer work so Sus wasn't alone. At times, when Naftali came into the stable to visit his beloved Sus, he saw him bowing his head against the horse on his left or his right, and it seemed to Naftali that Sus was listening to stories told him by the other horses or silently telling his own horsy story. It's true that horses cannot speak, but God's creatures can make themselves understood without words.

That winter Naftali wrote many stories—his own and those he heard from Reb Falik. He set them in type and printed them on his hand press. At times, when the sun shone over the silvery snow, Naftali hitched Sus and another horse to a sleigh and made a trip through the nearby towns to sell his storybooks or give them away to those who couldn't afford to buy them. Sometimes Reb Falik went along with him. They slept at inns and spent time with merchants, landowners, and Hasidim on their way to visit their rabbis' courts. Each one had a story to tell and Naftali either wrote them down or fixed them in his memory.

The winter passed and Naftali couldn't remember how. On Passover, Reb Falik's sons, daughters, and grandchildren came to celebrate the holiday at the estate, and again Naftali heard wondrous tales of Warsaw, Cracow, and even of Berlin, Paris, and London. The kings waged wars, but scientists made all kinds of discoveries and inventions. Astronomers discovered stars, planets, comets. Archaeologists dug out ruins of ancient cities. Chemists found new elements. In all the countries, tracks were being laid for railroad trains. Museums, libraries, and theaters were being built. Historians uncovered writings from generations past. The writers in every land described the life and the people among whom they dwelled. Mankind could not and would not forget its past. The history of the world grew ever richer in detail.

That spring something happened that Naftali had been expecting and, therefore, dreading. Sus became sick and stopped grazing. The sun shone outside, and Naftali led Sus out to pasture where the fresh green grass and many flowers sprouted. Sus sat down in the sunshine, looked at the grass and the flowers, but no longer grazed. A stillness shone out from his eyes, the tranquillity of a creature that has lived out its years and is ready to end its story on earth.

One afternoon, when Naftali went out to check on his beloved Sus, he saw that Sus was dead. Naftali couldn't hold back his tears. Sus had been a part of his life.

Naftali dug a grave for Sus not far from the old oak where Sus had died, and he buried him there. As a marker over the grave, he thrust into the ground the whip that he had never used. Its handle was made of oak.

Oddly enough, several weeks later Naftali noticed that the whip had turned into a sapling. The handle had put down roots into the earth where Sus lay and it began to sprout leaves. A tree grew over Sus, a new oak which drew sustenance from Sus's body. In time young branches grew out of the tree and birds sang upon them and built their nests there. Naftali could hardly bring himself to believe that this old dried-out stick had possessed enough life within it to grow and blossom. Naftali considered it a miracle. When the tree grew thicker, Naftali carved Sus's name into the bark along with the dates of his birth and death.

Yes, individual creatures die, but this doesn't end the story of the world. The whole earth, all the stars, all the planets, all the comets, represent within them one divine history, one source of life, one endless and wondrous story that only God knows in its entirety.

A few years afterward, Reb Falik died, and years later, Naftali the storyteller died. By then he was famous for his storybooks not only throughout Poland but in other countries as well. Before his death Naftali asked that he be buried beneath the young oak that had grown over Sus's grave and whose branches touched the old oak. On

Naftali's tombstone were carved these words from the Scriptures:

> LOVELY AND PLEASANT IN THEIR LIVES,
> AND IN THEIR DEATH
> THEY WERE NOT DIVIDED

LIBRARY OF CONGRESS
CATALOGING-IN-PUBLICATION DATA

Singer, Isaac Bashevis, 1904–
Shrewd Todie and Lyzer the Miser & other children's
stories/Isaac Bashevis Singer; illustrated by Margot Zemach.
—1st Barefoot Books ed. p. cm.—
(Little Barefoot Books)
Contents: Shrewd Todie and Lyzer the Miser—Tsirtsur and
Peziza—Utzel and his daughter Poverty—Menaseh's dream
—When Shlemiel went to Warsaw—Lemel and Tzipa—
The cat who thought she was a dog and the dog who
thought he was a cat
—Naftali the storyteller and his horse, Sus.
ISBN 1-56957-927-X (acid-free paper)
1. Jews—Poland—Juvenile fiction. 2. Children's stories,
American. [1. Jews—Poland—Fiction. 2. Poland—
Fiction. 3. Short stories.] I. Zemach, Margot,
ill. II. Title. III. Series.
PZ7.S6167Sh 1994 93-47364
[Fic]—dc20 CIP
AC

LITTLE BAREFOOT BOOKS

Alice's Adventures in Wonderland
by Lewis Carroll
Illustrated by John Tenniel

The Brownies' Merry Adventures
Written and illustrated
by Palmer Cox

A Child's Garden of Verses
by Robert Louis Stevenson
Illustrated by Charles Robinson

Fairy Tales of the World
Retold and illustrated
by Edmund Dulac

*How the Leopard Got His Spots
and Other Just So Stories*
by Rudyard Kipling
Illustrated by Rudyard Kipling
and Joseph M. Gleeson

The Light Princess
by George MacDonald
Illustrated by Arthur Hughes

A Little Book of Nonsense:
The Best of Edward Lear
Illustrated by the author

Rootabaga Stories
by Carl Sandburg
Illustrated by Maud Petersham
and Miska Petersham

Shrewd Todie and Lyzer the Miser
by Isaac Bashevis Singer
Illustrated by Margot Zemach

Whereyouwantogoto
and Other Unlikely Tales
by E. Nesbit
Illustrated by H. R. Millar
and Claude A. Shepperson

The Wizard of Oz
by L. Frank Baum
Illustrated by W. W. Denslow

The World Is Round
by Gertrude Stein
Illustrated by Roberta Arenson